Kick it in!

Written by Charlotte Guillain

Collins

Nat can kick it.

Nat kicks it in!

Nip in the gap.

Kim pops it in!

5

Dom nips to it.

I got it in!

Sam nips to it.

Kam can tap it.

Go and tap it.

Tim pops it in!

Kat pops in a sack.

Kat can go in it!

14

❧ After reading ❧

Letters and Sounds: Phase 2

Word count: 50

Focus phonemes: /c/ /k/, ck

Common exception words: the, to, I, go, and

Curriculum links: Physical Development

Early learning goals: Reading: read and understand simple sentences; use phonic knowledge to decode regular words and read them aloud accurately; read some irregular words

Developing fluency

- Your child may enjoy hearing you read the book.
- Encourage your child to read the text with emphasis, adding excitement to the exclamations as if they are watching the game, or are the player.

Phonic practice

- Point to the word **kicks** on page 3. Ask your child sound out and then blend the word. (*k/i/ck/s* – **kicks**)
- Turn to page 12. Ask your child to find two spellings for the /k/ sound. If necessary support them by pointing to **Kat** and **sack**.
- Look at the "I spy sounds" pages (14–15). Point to the cat and say: "I spy a /c/ in cat." Challenge your child to point to and name different things they can see containing the /c/ sound. Help them to identify /c/ items, asking them to repeat the word and listen out for the /c/ sound. (*court, coat, crumbs, cap, car, cows, cake, coach*)

Extending vocabulary

- Turn to page 5 and discuss the meaning of **pops**. Ask your child what other words could be used instead. (e.g. *puts, gets, chucks, throws*)
- On page 6, discuss what is meant by **nips**. Ask your child what other words could be used instead. (e.g. *runs, sprints, hurries*) Ask them to read the sentence with their suggested word to make sure it makes sense.